This

Nature Storybook

belongs to:

For Leah Li En with love, Nana. SW

For Claire, Cher and Betty, the liveliest Nanas I know. CJ

First published in 2022
by Walker Books Australia Pty Ltd
Locked Bag 22, Newtown
NSW 2042 Australia
www.walkerbooks.com.au

This edition published in 2023.

The moral rights of the author and illustrator have been asserted.

Text © 2022 Sue Whiting
Illustrations © 2022 Cate James

All rights reserved. No part of this publication may be reproduced, stored in a retrieval system, or transmitted in any form or by any means – electronic, mechanical, photocopying, recording or otherwise – without the prior written permission of the publisher.

A catalogue record for this book is available from the National Library of Australia

ISBN: 978 1 760656 26 3

The illustrations for this book were created digitally

Typeset in ITC Mendoza Roman and Polymer

Printed and bound in China

2 4 6 8 10 9 7 5 3 1

Walker Books acknowledges the Traditional Owners of the country on which we work, the Gadigal and Wangal peoples of the Eora Nation, and recognises their continuing connection to the land, waters and culture. We pay our respect to their Elders past and present.

THE ECHIDNA NEAR MY PLACE

Sue Whiting

Cate James

WALKER BOOKS
AND SUBSIDIARIES
LONDON • BOSTON • SYDNEY • AUCKLAND

There's a paddock at the end of my street. It's not a paddock like on a farm with cows and sheep. It's a scrubby paddock that climbs up the mountain to where the hang-gliders jump off and fly into the sky.

Nana and I walk through the paddock most days. And you know what? An echidna lives here. We don't always see it. But I'm always looking for it.

The short-beaked echidna is one of the oldest surviving mammals on the planet.

It lives in many different environments – forests, snowy mountains, deserts, grasslands and even in bushy patches and parklands in towns and cities.

Echidnas are very well camouflaged and are often difficult to spot.

Today is hot. The cicadas are so loud they are making my ears hurt. I thought the echidna would be hiding in the cool somewhere, but it's not.

It's crunching across the dry leaves.

I don't think the echidna knows about the hang-gliders. It's looking down, long nose like a stick to the ground, poking about the leaves and grasses, pink tongue flicking. Nana sees it too. We crouch beside it.

The echidna's snout is hairless and is usually about seven to eight centimetres long. It is used when foraging for food to break into rotten logs and termite mounds.

When the weather is warm, echidnas will forage in the cool of the mornings and afternoons.

The echidna scrambles downhill – up and over rocks and logs, under bushes, through piles of crackling leaves, scratching about in the dirt. It's covered in spikes, as if someone has stuck toothpicks all over its back, and it is far too prickly for hugs, that's for sure.

We follow it, but not too close. Every now and then it stops and looks behind. We stop too and pretend to be trees.

Echidnas have pointy spines all over their backs and short stubby tails. Their spines are about five centimetres long and are very sharp. You should never try to touch or pick up an echidna as you could injure it. And, although the spines are not poisonous, they could cause an infection.

And guess what the echidna does next? It plods out of the paddock and onto the road! Maybe it's trying to escape from the cicada noise.

The road isn't a busy one, but I'm worried for the echidna. Nana and I walk slowly behind it to protect it from cars. We're its bodyguards.

"Where do you think you're going?"
Nana asks the echidna.
It doesn't answer, of course.

The echidna doesn't have many enemies in the natural world. Its main threats come from dogs, eagles, dingoes and being hit by cars.

Echidnas are solitary animals. That means they live alone for most of the year, only finding other echidnas during the mating season. They usually have a large territory that they ramble through. Sometimes their territories overlap.

The echidna has a wobbly walk, as if it is walking on the deck of a swaying boat.

Its back feet look like they've been put on backwards!

They drag against the black tar of the road. I hope it doesn't hurt.

The echidna's legs are very short. The front legs have sharp claws, which are used for digging and ripping open termite mounds.

Its back legs point backwards. This helps the echidna shove the soil out of the way when burrowing. It has two claws on each back foot that it uses to groom itself.

"Maybe it's coming to our place," says Nana. And you know what? It is!

It climbs up a grassy patch and into our garden. My heart thumps in my chest. Nana films the echidna with her phone.

Echidnas are very shy and cautious animals with calm natures.

Despite their shyness, echidnas often wander through urban yards and can live near humans.

If an echidna enters your yard, it is important to keep any pet dogs inside or out of sight. Just the presence of a dog could cause the echidna to become stressed.

And you won't believe what the echidna does next – it walks right up our steps to our front door. True.

"That's not something you see every day," whispers Nana.

"Should we invite it in for an afternoon snack?" I whisper back.

"Termite tea and honey ant pie?" says Nana.

"And worm waffles," I add.

"And … and … ant-e-lope!" Nana's getting a little carried away.

The echidna pokes its nose inside. I hold my breath. Imagine an echidna coming to visit!

Echidnas eat termites, ants, worms and beetles. They catch their food with their long, thin tongues. Their tongues flick in and out very quickly and trap their prey with their sticky saliva. They often swallow lots of dirt at the same time!

But the echidna mustn't like our house-y smell, or maybe it doesn't know that Nana was joking about the antelope, because it turns around and lumbers back down the stairs, across the lawn and onto the road.

"Maybe it just wanted to see where you live," Nana says and puts her arm across my shoulders.

Echidnas have a very keen sense of smell that helps them to locate food and to find other echidnas in the mating season. It also helps them to detect danger.

We follow the echidna back to the paddock. It waddles across a wooden plank, over a puddle, then under a bush and disappears.

I'm a bit disappointed. Then, just as we turn to head home to have an afternoon snack without the echidna, we see it again. It has found a termite mound. It did want a snack!

Echidnas have tiny mouths at the very end of their snouts, on the underside. They don't have any teeth, so they grind food between their tongues and the bottoms of their mouths.

They eat about 40,000 ants and termites a day!

I squeal with excitement and get a little too close.

The echidna stops. It hides its snout and makes itself round like a soccer ball. A spiky one. The spikes flare out.

I step back. "Sorry," I say.

When scared or disturbed, an echidna hides rather than fights. It will tuck in its legs and snout and curl itself into a ball, with its spikes sticking out in a threatening way. That's usually enough to frighten off most threats!

It will also hide between rocks or burrow into the soil to escape from predators such as dogs or eagles. Its powerful arms and claws allow it to dig itself into the ground swiftly, leaving only a mound of scary-looking spikes sticking out.

We stay really still and soon the echidna is off again. Faster this time, and into some thick bushes. Nana and I wait for ages, but it doesn't come out, so we go home.

No echidna. But a great story to tell Dad at dinner tonight.

When resting, echidnas shelter in hollow logs or stumps, in rocky crevices or in burrows.

Echidnas are one of the few animals in Australia that hibernate. Echidnas in Tasmania and in the Australian Alps may hibernate for up to six months.

INFORMATION ABOUT THE SHORT-BEAKED ECHIDNA

The short-beaked echidna is very common throughout Australia and in parts of Papua New Guinea. Like the platypus, it is a monotreme – an egg-laying mammal. The female echidna lays only one egg at a time. She carries it in her pouch for about ten days until it hatches. The baby echidna is called a puggle and is born blind and hairless. It stays in the pouch for about three months, suckling milk through the skin inside its mother's pouch. When the puggle starts to grow spines, the mother will push it out of her pouch and build it a burrow to shelter in. The puggle will start to eat ants and termites but will also suckle milk until it is about six or seven months old. When fully developed, the mother will open the burrow, feed her puggle one last time and then leave it to look after itself.

INDEX

ants 18, 23, 28
ball 24
burrow 14, 24, 27, 28
camouflage 7
claws 14, 24
dig 14, 24
feet 14
food 8, 18, 21, 23
hibernate 27
legs 14, 24
live 6, 7, 13, 17, 21
mammal 7, 28
mating 13, 21
monotreme 28
puggle 28
sharp 11, 14
smell 21
snout 8, 23, 24
spikes 10, 24
spines 11, 28
termite ...8, 14, 18, 22, 23, 28
territory 13
threats 13, 24
tongue 8, 18, 23

Look up the pages to find out about these echidna things.
Don't forget to look at both kinds of words – **this kind** and this kind.

ABOUT THE AUTHOR

Sue Whiting is a children's author and editor. She has written books for all ages, including the bestselling *Missing*, the award-winning *A Swim in the Sea* and the CBCA Notable Books, *Platypus*, *Get a Grip Cooper Jones* and *Beware the Deep Dark Forest*. As a schools' performer, Sue has informed, inspired and entertained thousands of kids across the country. Sue lives in a small coastal village south of Sydney, and has often had echidnas waddle through her yard.

ABOUT THE ILLUSTRATOR

Cate James is an award-winning illustrator from the Northern Beaches of Sydney, where she lives among trees, surrounded by birds and possums. She is also a printmaker, arts educator, children's hospital arts volunteer and print technician at the University of New South Wales. Cate was illustrator-in-residence at the Royal Hospital for Sick Children in Edinburgh before moving to Australia. To relax and to think up ideas for her work, she loves swimming in ocean pools and walks with Sebastian, her miniature sausage dog.